PUFFIN BOOKS

Frank Rodgers has written and illustrated a wide range of books for children – picture books, story books, non-fiction and novels. His children's stories have been broadcast on radio and TV and he has created a sitcom series for CBBC based on his book *The Intergalactic Kitchen*. His recent work for Puffin includes the *Eyetooth* books and the bestselling *Witch's Dog* and *Robodog* titles. He was an art teacher before becoming an author and illustrator and lives in Glasgow with his wife. He has two grown-up children.

A is for AAARGH!

FRANK RODGERS

PUFFIN

PUFFIN BOOKS

Published by the Penguin Group
Penguin Books Ltd, 80 Strand, London WC2R 0RL, England
Penguin Group (USA), Inc., 375 Hudson Street, New York, New York 10014, USA
Penguin Books Australia Ltd, 250 Camberwell Road, Camberwell, Victoria 3124, Australia
Penguin Books Canada Ltd, 10 Alcorn Avenue, Toronto, Ontario, Canada M4V 3B2
Penguin Books India (P) Ltd, 11 Community Centre, Panchsheel Park, New Delhi – 110 017, India
Penguin Books (NZ) Ltd, Cnr Rosedale and Airborne Roads, Albany, Auckland, New Zealand
Penguin Books (South Africa) (Pty) Ltd, 24 Sturdee Avenue, Rosebank 2196, South Africa

Penguin Books Ltd, Registered Offices: 80 Strand, London WC2R 0RL, England

www.penguin.com

First published 2004
1 3 5 7 9 10 8 6 4 2

Set in 15/22pt Times New Roman Schoolbook

The moral right of the author/illustrator has been asserted

Printed in China by Midas Printing Ltd

British Library Cataloguing in Publication Data
A CIP catalogue record for this book is available from the British Library

ISBN 0–141–31562–8

"This is Miss Snitchell," said the Head
Teacher to Class Three. "She will be
taking you while your own teacher is
off ill."

The Head Teacher turned to Miss
Snitchell and whispered, "I'm afraid
this is the worst class in the school."
    "Don't worry," Miss Snitchell
whispered back. "I know how to deal
with rascals."

The Head Teacher left and "Beasty" Barrett, the class bully, grinned and nudged his nasty pal, "Biff" Higson.

"Let's have some fun with this one," he hissed.

The rest of the class heard this and giggled. *This could be good*, they thought.

Miss Snitchell cleared her throat.

"Now children," she began, "we'll start with an alphabet exercise to test your vocabulary."

Beasty turned to Biff and winked.

"She thinks we're babies," he said. "Alphabet exercise? Hah! She's a pushover!"

"Who will give me an example to begin with?" said Miss Snitchell. "A is for …?"

"AAAARGH!"

gurgled Beasty, falling backwards.

The class roared with laughter. Beasty was up to his tricks again!

Miss Snitchell smiled faintly. She could take a joke.

"Remove your arrow, boy, and put it away," she said when the laughter had subsided.

Miss Snitchell looked around and continued. "B is for …?" she said.

"BOO!"

yelled Biff, jumping
up from his seat.
"Sit down!" said Miss Snitchell sternly.
Biff sat down, grinning smugly.

Miss Snitchell looked
around the class
again. "C is for
centipede," she
said quickly
before she could
be interrupted.

"That's right, miss!" shouted Beasty.

"C is for centipede … which is a creepy-crawly like my pet spider."

Beasty set his spider free on the desktop. The spider scuttled down a chair leg and set off across the floor.

Much to Beasty's disappointment his hairy little pet disappeared down a crack in the floorboards.

"Now sit down and pay attention," called Miss Snitchell. **"Please!"**

The children sat down and smiled.

This was good fun. When everything was quiet Miss Snitchell began again.

"D is for deplorable," she said sharply, pointing at Beasty, "which is what your behaviour has been, young man."

Beasty smiled angelically.

The class tittered.

"Now," went on Miss Snitchell, the class quiet once more, "we will continue."

"E is for EEEEK!"
she cried in surprise as a rat ran along
the floor and jumped onto one of her
shoes.

Biff Higson, amid screams of laughter
from the class, ran over and picked it up.

12

"Sorry, miss," he said, grinning, as he put it in his pocket. "It's my pet rat, Ronnie. He escaped."

Miss Snitchell rapped on the desk for silence. She looked quite stern.

"F is for fright, which is what I got from your pet rat," she said to Biff. The class laughed and Miss Snitchell continued. "G is for grandmother," she said, "which is what I am. I have two good-looking grandsons, about your age. They are the top goalscorers in their school team.

"Here is a picture of them holding the Schools' Championship Cup."

The boys were impressed and the girls smiled. But Biff glowered at Beasty.

"She's better than I thought," he muttered.

"Just wait," hissed Beasty. "We haven't finished with her yet!"

16

"Now," said Miss Snitchell, "back to the alphabet. H is for?"

"Handsome," said good-looking Jim Peters from the back.

The other boys rolled their eyes and the girls smiled again.

"Good," said Miss Snitchell.

"H is for horror!" said Beasty. "I love horror films."

"Do you now?" said Miss Snitchell. "Do you really …?" She trailed off and looked at Beasty in an odd way. Beasty grinned and nodded. Miss Snitchell continued. "I is for …?"

"ICKYPOO!"

sniggered Biff loudly.

The class giggled.

"That's enough!" snapped Miss
Snitchell. "J is for jungle and jack-in-
the-box and juggernaught. K is for …?"

"King Kong!"

bellowed Beasty, lumbering around
like an ape.

The class laughed
again, encouraging Beasty and Biff.

"L is for Leopard-Man!" snarled Biff, growling and clawing at the girls. "And M is for monster movies!"

"Yeh … M is for Mummy!" shouted
Beasty, winding a scarf round his face.
"The Mummy from the Tomb!"
he wailed.

"N is for . . . **nasty!"**

yelled Biff, throwing his books in the air.

The class was now in uproar.

Miss Snitchell shouted but her voice couldn't be heard.

"O is for 'orrible! Like what I am!"
yelled Beasty gleefully, jumping on top of
a desk. From there he controlled the class
just like the conductor of an orchestra.

24

He raised his hand.
"P is for …?"
    "Putrid!"
yelled the class.
    "Q is for …?"
    "Quicksand!"
they shouted.

"R is for …?"
"Rotten!"
"S is for …?"
"Slime!"
"T is for …?"

"Terrified!"

Miss Snitchell seemed to give up.
She slumped forwards on her desk.
The class looked at her curiously,
with evil little grins.

They wanted Miss Snitchell to watch them. It would be no fun if she didn't. They were so enjoying themselves.

A muffled sound came from the teacher's desk.

"Heh, heh, she's cracked," said Beasty with a smirk.

They gathered round her desk and
listened to Miss Snitchell as she spoke
into her arms. "U is for ..." she whispered.

"Louder, miss!" they shouted
gleefully. "We can't hear you, miss!"
They listened again.

"U …" said Miss Snitchell, her voice slightly muffled by her arms, "is for …

UUUURGH!"

The class was startled. Uuuuurgh?
Was that a word?

Miss Snitchell was going on, her
voice growing louder and stronger.

"V is for vampire!"

The class looked at one another.

"Ha, ha," said Beasty, "Miss Snitchell got the joke."

The class started to laugh but stopped suddenly as Miss Snitchell raised her head.

"W," she said, "is for . . .

WEREWOLF!"

The class gasped. The game was definitely over. Miss Snitchell had changed. Her little bird-like face was hairy and had a pointed nose, ears and dripping fangs.

Miss Snitchell was a werewolf! Couldn't she take a joke?

But Miss Snitchell didn't look at all
in the mood for laughs. She rose slowly,
her red eyes blazing.

"X is for my signature," she hissed

and scratched a big X on the board with
one of her long, sharp, black nails.
SCREEEEEEK!
The class moaned.

Miss Snitchell's eyes narrowed. "Y is for yeti," she snarled, holding up a snapshot.

"My hairy monster friend from the Himalayas."

The class stared open-mouthed, goggle-eyed.

Beasty and Biff turned a lovely shade of pink as Miss Snitchell's hairy finger pointed at them …

… and then to the rest of the class.

"And finally," she growled, "Z is for zombie! And all of you will be as watchful as zombies from now on when I teach you. Do you understand?"

The class gulped and nodded together. They understood.

"Now," said Miss Snitchell, "as you all seem to be fond of monsters and horror stories each of you can write out an alphabet for me for tomorrow morning …

a HORRIBLE alphabet … starting with A is for AAAARGH!" She grinned wickedly at Biff and Beasty who slid down in their seats. The interval bell rang but nobody moved.

Miss Snitchell lifted up her hairy
snout to the ceiling and gave a long,
piercing, triumphant howl.

Just then the Head Teacher came in.
The class looked at the Head Teacher.
The Head Teacher looked at Miss
Snitchell, then at the class.

Miss Snitchell smiled sweetly.

"I'm pleased to see that Class Three behaved themselves," said the Head Teacher.

"Oh, yes," replied Miss Snitchell, "they were little angels." She turned to the class and her eyes twinkled mischievously …

"Class dismissed," she said.